CW00419108

the other place

By Rayne Havok

By: Rayne Havok

Cover art by: Rayne Havok

This is a work of fiction, if you find any similarities what- so- ever they are coincidental.

Warning:

May offend

preface

I had a dream once; I was running through a field of grass and wild flowers, spinning and loving every minute. The vivid colors took my breath. A cut scene, like how one sequence fades into another. Red, wet and warm--I was completely covered in blood. At first, I was nervous it was my own, but once I realized it wasn't a smile crept across my face.

I looked around and the flowers had transformed into bodies--a field of fresh dead bodies. Oozing, dripping and spirting geysers of blood. I had a warm feeling of home but it also excited me as nothing ever had.

I woke, covered in a slick dampness that I traced to between my legs. My young pussy was soaked. And that had told me all I needed to know about who I was.

one

Oh my god, like, could my mother have been literally *anything* else in this world? Lame ass psychic reading shop slash old crusty bookstore is all she leaves me in the world.

"Eew," I mutter aloud when the container of some bull shit essential oil leaks out onto my hand and contaminates me.

She was the most *out there* person, unable to give me anything normal in life, including my name. I'm named after Sean Penn, and if it weren't bad enough having a boy's name, she spelled it Sian. Teachers trying to pronounce it on the first day of school reminded me at least once a year just how different she really was. *So annoying*.

She had told me once, after overhearing me complain about it, that the alternative was Brenda. So, great, I'm either the most obscure name or the most basic bitch. I might have died at birth if I had been forced into the role of a Brenda. So, here I am, Sian, the new owner of a tarot shop with no idea how to really read cards or what to do to make people come in here, and the people skills of a rabid monkey in a cage. I can't imagine this won't be profitable. *Eye roll*.

My mother and I never really got each other, but there were a lot of years when I was a child that I'd sit and watch her read people. She loved tarot and she loved talking to people. She loved lifting their spirits when they were sad and looking for hope, she had a gift for giving them promises of love and an ever after.

I can't be bothered with the fake and hopeful. I live my life in the reality that it is, I have no patients for people who want all the fairytales--the ones *before* the happily ever after's were traded for the endings instead of the horror that used to finalize them. I am not a romantic. And I can't fathom running this place and it being anything sustainable for me if that's the clientele in my future.

I move around the shop, touching and holding things, trying to remember if I've learned their purpose and the reason for them.

For the most part, I feel capable of being able to bumble my way through some readings with the one off'ers. The people who haven't paid a fortune to the tellers for years already-the ones my mother actually prided herself on collecting.

Nope, probably not going to be able to dupe them. But that desperate lady, making me her last resort, or the drunk frat boys looking to joke around, even the desperate man who just lost his job and finds me for reassurances. Maybe those are my new clientele.

The next few hours are spent rearranging the shop into something more functional for me. Which mostly means I've hidden away all the things I have no use for or can't answer questions about if someone were looking to inquire about such things. It's not as barren as I thought it might be, I do actually have a basic handle on this stuff. The old books would likely sell themselves, the oils and trinkets are for anyone really. And me, at the table with a crystal ball my mother called an orbuculum, and a deck of tarot cards, should finish the authenticity of this place just fine.

It doesn't look too different from how mom left it, but it will be a whole different thing entirely while I'm here in charge of it. Hopefully, I can keep afloat so I won't lose what I have already made of myself on this earth so far before undertaking this thing.

Had I not lost my boyfriend recently, and my mother just before that, I may not have even attempted this, but when all the resources in your life dry up, you must pick up that lemon and squeeze, I guess?

Unlike my mother, my boyfriend did not die. *Unfortunately*. He's just another one for ex pile- one more notch on my loser belt. Elle can have him, she's better at handling garbage than I am anyway. I'm sure they're going to make great fucking children together.

So, until something happens in my life to perk up my financial status, I must tell the fortunes of the unfortunate.

two

Day one of this little 'adventure', some asshole may call it, went as slow as anyone could have anticipated. Surprisingly, a couple of teen girls came in and looked for just a minute while I stood cross armed, ready to answer whatever questions they had- assuming it was going to be some witchcraft shit to get a boy to like them. Alas, they never spoke, not even to each other.

The silence is a bit too much so I turn the music up and let it be heard through the speakers, if only for my own entertainment.

The smells are something that always reminded me of my mom. I could smell, before I'd hear her come home at night. Independently, all of them are distinct, but together they make kind of an aura of smell, something so faint and undefinable that you can't really pinpoint what it is you're smelling. It's not too bad actually. That's not saying that I'm becoming ok with this whole thing. I'm not. It just doesn't give me a headache like I thought it might.

I close the shop after getting everything tidy for the morning and head home. It's late and I'm beat. There's very little that makes me more tired than doing nothing all day.

I hope it's not going to be like this for long.

My mother hadn't needed to advertise for quite a long time, she was just known for her gifts. I may have to though, to get some fresh eyes on the town's new 'psychic girl'. I don't need much, just enough for bills and such. The building is on the lot my mother actually paid for, so I don't even have to save for that, just the utilities and annual property taxes are subtracted. My one bedroom apartment doesn't take much to keep out of eviction, either, so here's hoping for at least that much monthly.

Day two has been much better, I actually have a tarot reading scheduled for 2 pm, so hopefully I can muddle my way thorough that and get some cash. Maybe I'll recommend some shit for him to buy as well- although, that might be a bit aggressive for my second day.

My appointment shows up ten minutes early. On top of being punctual, he is young, mid 20's, tall and sheepish looking. He shoots his hand right out to me. "You must be Sian," he says with a grin on his face.

"I am, nice to meet you." I'm a little taken aback by the familiarity. He seems to notice and quickly goes on to say he's been in here a few times to talk with my mother.

I'm instantly thinking of a way to cancel this reading now, but before I can, he adds, "She was a little too serious for me, I was hoping to get the perspective of a younger person, actually. I thought it couldn't hurt anything to come in and chat for a minute. See if maybe any of your mom's gifts rubbed off on you."

I try my best to relax and play it cool, reaching inside to gather all the little things my mother would do and then applying them to my persona for authenticity. I lead him to the table, still not sure enough of my voice to speak without nerves. I pull out the chair meant for him and make my way to mine while he gets comfortable in the creaky wooden seat.

I fiddle with the table and take a deep breath. "What's your name?" I can't be sure if it was told to me or not, but when he says 'Brandon' apologetically, I know he had not shared it with me yet.

"Ok, Brandon, nice to meet you. I'm going to ask you some pretty basic questions, you'll answer them, and then I'll see what I see." I pull the clear ball toward me and begin to shuffle the large deck.

“Ok, sounds good.” He folds his hands on the table and waits patiently for me to begin.

I try to flush the nerves from my voice as I begin.

Laying the cards on the table as I’d observed my mother do all my life, I watch as he becomes interested in certain ones and make mental notes to expound upon them. After all, this is basically about reading someone’s unasked questions. That’s what makes it a psychic reading and not a therapy session. If you merely answer their questions, they can’t get those shivers that tell them you know something secret about them.

“Ok, Brandon, I have a sense that you’re having some troubles with love.”

“You could say that. But, quite frankly, couldn’t we all?” he chuffs.

"I suppose, but it looks like it's on your mind right now, want to ask anything specific?"

"Not yet. What else you got?"

His tone isn't skeptical or doubting, it sounds like he just wants to know what I can do. Honestly, I don't even know what I can do, so let's see.

"I suppose you were also wondering about your life in general. And it looks like it's going quite well from what I can see, nothing too dramatic at all," I guess.

His eyebrow lifts subtly from surprise. "That's all you're getting, huh? Nothing about winning the lottery? Kids? Marriage?... Death?"

A flicker of something in the ball, so quick I don't quite know what I saw. But my mind turns it into blood, a sharp, fiery, red, and vivid scene--Brandon standing in front of a neon sign with half his face slithering down his shoulder, leaving a trail of blood behind, his expression is neutral- even if it is from only one hemisphere.

I shake my head, trying to rid that and get back on track.

“What? Did you see something?” his eyes light up, “you saw something!”

Laughing, so nervously even I can hear it, I say, “no, nothing.” I try to giggle and pretend this was all something silly, but the look on his face tells me he is curious.

“Just a flash, nothing I can really say,” hopefully he doesn’t see my nervousness or confusion.

"Was it about the lottery?" his eager boyish charm makes me laugh.

"No, not that I could see."

"Shit, probably about how I'm gonna die then."

Just the mention of his death has me seeing it again, this time so clearly I can actually hear the sickening sounds being made when the sticky blood separates.

A shiver runs down my spine. I don't know how to recover from this so I just begin awkwardly collecting the cards and trying to make an excuse about a headache.

He looks as if he wants to contradict me, or even make me stay, but he doesn't, he just watches me. I can see the curiosity in his eyes, the little crinkles on the sides when he squints his doubt. I try to focus on getting him out of here, but he's not standing or making any progress whatsoever.

"Um, so, I won't charge you for this. Sorry. I have a condition," *I have no condition.* "It comes on quick, so you should just go."

He finally puts his hands on the table, tentatively, still not wanting to really go, nor believing that this doesn't have anything to do with him. When he finally stands, I try not to look at him making his way to the door.

I turn around only when I hear the door's chime.

He's still inside the shop.

Tricky bastard.

"I'd like to make another appointment with you, like after your *condition* is gone, or whatever."

"Ok, sounds good." I round the corner and press myself against the wall, standing there a full two minutes after I hear the door chime again. I peak around the corner to make sure he's actually gone this time. The shop is empty. Taking a deep breath to calm myself, I'm finally feeling a little more normal again.

That was fucking weird.

The cash on the table is more than enough to cover the reading, and also too much for what I've actually done for him. I tuck it in my pocket, however, and finish arranging everything.

Picking up the glass ball, I look at it and turn it over in my hands suspiciously. I've never seen anything in this before, just a misshapen version of my face or the lights around the room glowing back. Never. Ever. Anything like this before.

I look closer into it, trying to summon Brandon's slippery face looking at me, but nothing comes, so I set it back down.

I take a load off on the couch reserved for clients, set up like a waiting area, and rest my head on the back, closing my eyes for only a moment, but waking hours later when the sun has fallen and the room has gone dark.

Shit.

I rush out, locking the door behind me and practically run home. This has all been too much.

three

I unlock the front door to my apartment with shaking hands. I can't understand what I saw, nor the level of tiredness that overwhelmed me afterward. I'm so full of adrenaline now though. Energy is just flowing through me.

Pacing my small living room with enough vigor to wear out the carpet, I can't stop *feeling* what I saw in the ball. I'm wondering what it means. Will that be the way he dies?

My mother always said there was something in our family line that made us capable of seeing, or reading, things that most weren't. But she would also contradict that just as frequently. Could it be merely my sick mind warping something that was a figment of it to begin with?

That seems more likely to me. Mix equal parts, nerves and excitement, add in expectation, and just a dash of vivid imagination, you've got yourself 'crystal ball visions'.

I have nothing concrete that would direct me either way or even give me more options to go off of. No one to even ask such a question. So my mind reels.

It was pretty badass, don't get me wrong. I'm the queen of blood and guts and that was a horror show. So I'm not upset about that, but I am big on the *why* of things and can't get passed the reason for it.

Maybe a walk would do me some good.

Maybe a bottle of something would take the edge off.

I grab my jacket and practically bounce down the stairs and out the security door, headed for the corner liquor store that I know will be open this late.

As I approach, the glowing florescent bulbs remind me of the scene from earlier. I pause a moment to see if it could actually be the same spot it happened. Maybe I pulled the whole thing together in my mind from memories of being here before. But as I try and place all the colors and the position he'd have been standing, I know it can't be this place.

Before I can stop myself, I head in the same direction from which I'd come, and walk to the next one. Three miles later I'm in from of O'Neil's. It's closed now and the lights are off, I try to remember what it would look like if they were on and I can't even recall the color the bulbs would be.

Damn it.

That sucks, because now I have nothing to drink. And a long ass walk home- all for nothing. I meander back, not really regretting my wild goose chase, and somehow I'm finding relief that it can't be a memory of mine. So when I kick my door shut behind me, I rest a little easier knowing that I probably pulled that out of my ass and that poor nice Brandon will be fine.

Luckily, I have a swig of freezer vodka to put my mind at ease. I throw the empty bottle into the recycling bin and head for the living room, knowing that the hours I slept at the shop this afternoon would keep sleep away.

I pull my bra through my sleeve and kick my pants off, trying to relax, flicking through the channels, exhausting all my options before inevitably settling on a Netflix binge.

My thumb stops suddenly, hovering over the channel up button, a photo of Brandon the size of my screen is smiling at me.

What.

The.

Fuck.

…"reports say that Brandon Freeman was murdered earlier today outside this corner store, witnesses are quoted saying, 'a madman, wielding a machete, came out of nowhere and simply hacked him with it.'"

The reporter's face falls and she takes a deep breath before continuing. My attention remains holey engulfed by this.

""it was like, that's all he wanted. Like, he just came here to kill him,""" the teenage witness recounts.

The reporter continues, "it appears that the man walked up to Brandon with the intent to kill him and simply walked away after doing so, even passing other people on the way to his car." Looking down at a notecard she has in her hand, "A blue four door sedan, police have a bolo out for this car and the maniac driving it. We urge anyone who may come across this man, or a vehicle fitting this description to leave and call the police. Stay clear and stay vigilant folks."

The screen cuts to more footage of the scene- none of it Brandon obviously, but plenty of the storefront that happens to be *exactly* the image from the ball. And I've never been there. And he *is* dead. Like, for *real* dead. It wasn't clear on exactly where he was 'hacked', (the witness so gracefully described) but I know in my gut, it was right on the top of the head.

I don't really understand why the smile on my face is spread so wide it's making my cheeks hurt, so I chalk it up to morbid fascination and leave my fucked up head out of it.

Who am I kidding though? This is fucking crazy.

***

“Hey, aunt Farrah.”

“Oh, Sian! I’m so happy you called, how are things? I’ve been meaning to get in touch, but you know how it is with the kids and Ben. It’s really almost impossible to even use the bathroom without interruption.” She giggles her meek and oh-so-her signature embarrassed-to-be-so-happy chuckle before I even get to the reason for my call.

“I’m ok, I’ve been at the shop, moms shop, for a couple days.” I wait to hear what she’ll say about that without my leading her in any specific direction.

“Oh?” she pauses for a minute and I can almost see her wringing her hands.

“Yea.”

"How's it going? Is it hard to be there without her?"

"No, not really, I was actually just wondering if you believed in all the stuff in there," I say, trying to sound as blasé as possible.

"Well, I don't know that I believe it for myself, but your mama swore by it- her and your grandma both. I never really went into depth with either one of them as to what exactly they had. But I know it was something."

"Oh," I'm kind of let down that I can't get a grasp of what might have happened with Brandon the other night.

She must hear that I'm let down and jumps into one of her run-on stories, conspiratorially lowering her voice to get into gossip-mode. "I do know that once she told me not to hang out with this girl in third grade, she didn't tell me why. But I almost always did as she asked me. You know she was always so smart, and I just looked up to her. Anyway, it wasn't until 6th grade that I even remembered her saying anything about it. But that girl had a besties slumber party and some madman broke into her house through the open window and killed everyone. It was a bloodbath- eight little 6th grade girls lying in a heap. The parents slept through the whole thing. It was crazy. Carmen, your mama, she was crying and hugging me so hard, thanking me for never becoming friends with her back in 3rd grade, even though I had been so eager to try." Her voice starts to have a tremble in it. "I'd forgotten until then. But after that, I couldn't shake it off. And I couldn't ask or bring it up. Ever. It was all too much."

"Damn. That's heavy, Farrah. Did they ever catch the guy?"

"No. So we moved soon after that, your grandma never said a word, just one day all our things were packed and she said we were moving. So we did. Never looked back. But when there's a child killer out there, no one really wonders enough to ask it allowed."

I shake my head, this is a lot to hear, but I really am more curious than ever now. And she's the only one left in my family, so I don't think I'm ever going to know it all.

"What town was that?" I ask innocently enough so as not to trigger her suspicion.

"Sun Ville. It was such a good place," she goes off topic, "You know it only takes a beat to learn your life is momentary and fleeting. You have to make sure you live yours to the fullest. Your mama was too young." She sniffs back the tears that always come when she talks about her sister being dead.

"Sorry aunt Farrah, I know you loved her so much. I won't squander anything. I promise."

"Good for you Sian. Your mom had always been so proud of you. You're going to do such good things in your life, I just know it. Hopefully you can make something of that shop in your own image. Put your signature on it. I don't want to get too sappy, but you and your mom always looked like you made such a good team there."

I smile at my memories there with her; realizing quite a few are my favorites. My angsty teenage years kept me out of there altogether eventually, but she never let on that it bothered her, even though I could assume it had. She just let me be me for the most part.

I suppose if I'd known this shit with Brandon would happen I would have asked more or wondered more. But most people thought the whole thing was bullshit and I couldn't overlook that then.

"Thank you for reminding me of the good times there, Farrah. Will you send my love to the kids and Ben?"

"Of course, my sweet girl. Take care, honey."

"You too." I end the call and instantly google Sun Ville murders.

four

Ok, so from what I've gathered, Sun Ville had one hell of a time as a community after that incident. Those eight little girls died the night a man broke in through a window that the girls had left open in the first floor bedroom. The girls had been slaughtered- stabbed and completely brutalized, all while the parents of the girl had been asleep. The little brother went to the room in the morning to gather them all for breakfast and found the girls.

There is a 10 year update, a story of him retelling how he'd found them and that it had been so shocking he's never recovered.

The man has never been caught and yet the town never had another killing like it. It baffled many involved with the case, such a heinous crime is usually just one of many. It was thought the maniac was caught for another crime, or dead.

I have to believe that my mother had obviously seen a vision of what had happened which is what inevitably saved my aunt.

She never used the orbuculum, so I don't think she saw it in the ball like I had, maybe the cards told her. Maybe she just had a paranoid dream that she couldn't overlook. I can't know, and I *will* never know.

That's annoying.

What I do know is this shit is real, really real. And I guess by the look of it, I could probably have changed what happened to Brandon if I had spoken up. I suppose I should feel guilty for not doing so, but I couldn't have had an idea it was real. From everything I knew about my mother, she was 'sensitive' (her word) to the world, I never got the impression that there were visions or any truth behind her 'sensitivity'.

I don't even know if I'm clear whether it *is* the same as my mom. And if I could have even done something, is it even my responsibility to inform them? Should a person even know that they're going to die, or how? Is it all mapped out and maybe there are consequences for stopping such a plan simply to alleviate one's burden of conscience? I don't know.

What I do know, is I have something inside of me now to know exactly what the fuck *is* going on with death beforehand. I need to know if I could have changed this, and, if so, what would the outcome have been?

It doesn't seem like my aunt has had any life altering consequences happen to her for escaping her death. But then, my mom had to put a stop to it before the possibility ever happened. What could I have stopped for Brandon to not go the store that night? What led to that? It's impossible to guess.

Somehow, my mom figured out that never being friends with that girl in the first place was what it took. If my aunt had become friends with her and simply not gone to that slumber party, would it all have happened another time, a different way? Possibly.

So, in order to test these ideas, I need to get to work, but first, I need to get a reason to go to work. I quickly make a post advertising that I have some fantastic powers and not only that but, surprisingly, I have openings.

"Come see me see you."

After communicating with a few potential people online, I actually get someone in the door. She is younger lady, cute pixie cut blonde with big blue eyes, eager to hear all I know about her.

We sit at the table, my crystal ball in the center, making it my focal point. I don't shuffle the tarot deck, I don't do anything else. I just start asking her questions.

She answers them without hesitation. She has a boyfriend, they are happy; she wants to know if he's faithful. I get nothing from the ball, but I tell her he's faithful because she looks too meek to handle if I told her something else.

She wants to know if she will be rich –I tell her she will be comfortable. I ask her what her boyfriend David does for a living and she tells me he's in finance, whatever that means.

"Will we live a long life together?"

A flash, there it is.

"Tell me what David looks like."

She describes a tall, dark haired man. The description works for who I see. And it's actually more clear than my first vision. It lasts a few moments. From what I can tell, her boyfriend is *definitely* not a keeper.

He pulls her back with a fist full of her hair, slams her onto her back- blood pooling quickly around her head. She's still alive though and scrambles to get up- making it a few feet on her hands and knees before he gets to her again. He pounces on her back as if he's riding a horse and she collapses. Driving his fist into her head over and over until finally grinding her face into the carpet of her stylish living room. The last thing that I get is the refreshing sound of him opening a beer and leaning against the counter with blood-covered hands.

My arms are full of goosebumps, the hair on the back of my neck standing up. It's strange to see such a thing. I'd never seen anyone die before, even Brandon was somehow less brutal than this because of the visceral effect I'm having knowing she will absolutely be dead soon.

I keep quiet for too long, I can't really speak yet.

I do want to warn her, which is the least I can do. If I want to figure out if I can stop things from happening, I need to calmly ask her to avoid him, and hope she listens. Then, I'll have some definitive information to go on.

"So, has David done anything that would make you believe he was abusive?"

Her face changes a little, "well, like sometimes he gets stressed out, his work is really hard, long hours..." she seems to lose her steam. "Yea, I guess you could say that," she says bluntly.

"Why are you with him?" I ask, because seriously, what the fuck.

"He's really good at apologizing." I can tell she is upset with herself for accepting his behavior even though she knows he's manipulating her.

"You want me to sugar coat this? I can, if you want."

"Just tell me, did you see something?"

I nod.

"Tell me."

"He's going to kill you. And like not in a quick way either. He fucking *murders* you."

Her hands shake as she reaches into her bag and pulls out a tissue. She wipes under her eyes and it reveals a black eye she had covered with makeup. “I was hoping he had changed this time. That’s really why I’m here, I needed to know if he had. I don’t know how you knew, or even if it is true, but it’s enough for me to follow through with my contingency plan. I’m not staying with him. I’m leaving.”

I feel relief, and I little stressed, I hope I haven’t done anything wrong by telling her. But I need to do this in order to know what I’m capable of controlling and if I am able to change the outcome of what could be destiny.

“I hope you do. It doesn’t look good for you if you stay.”

“Do you have a restroom I can use?”

I point her to the small powder room and she sneaks off.

She's making a phone call, but I can't discern anything other than murmurs.

She comes out and thanks me for helping her, hands me a wad of cash I don't count, but do thank her for, and then takes a deep breath, hesitating with her hand on the exit door. "It gets that bad, huh?"

"It gets worse than you could imagine. He's a horrible person."

She leaves with a nod but not another word. I go to the door and lock it, taking a few minutes to myself on the couch, knowing last time sleep rushed in.

I close my eyes.

Shelby's living room is dark, I cannot make anything out but somehow I know I'm with her, maybe the smell--it's her perfume. She walks in the door, wearing the outfit from today, I remember because the blouse is full of vivid flowers, and a pair of black jeans.

The door closes behind her just as she hits the light switch. The brightness is instant. She walks right passed me and into the kitchen without a word. Setting the bags on the counter, she begins putting them away. The front door creeks open and I turn to see who has entered but the hood from his sweater is covering too much of his face. He walks confidently into the kitchen and I'm left standing in the doorway watching.

He slides open a drawer, Shelby still hasn't acknowledged him, she doesn't even notice when he pulls large knife out. I hold my breath as he lifts the blade high over his head and brings it down into her shoulder. Only then does Shelby seem to notice something is amiss.

Her shirt quickly takes on a red hue and she collapses to the floor.

Now we are all in her bedroom, she is strapped to the large bed, naked and squirming. I'm standing in the doorway, although I didn't get here on my own, and when I try to move my feet I'm unable to lift them, they weigh too much.

The hooded man, steps toward the bed and Shelby screams, pulling hard at her restraints, I can see the damage they are doing to her wrists and ankles. I wince.

He pounces on top of her, blade in his hand and quickly makes slices across her skin. I hear the unreal and exaggerated movie sounds of the knife moving.

Shing shing

He jumps off the mattress and reaches for the top of her head, pulling hard at her hair until I hear the wet sound of him pulling her face off. The breath hitches in my lungs, unable to breathe the entire time he's pulling at her. Yanking it down her chest. Her belly. Her legs. Until she is skinless and little beads of blood droplets begin trickling.

The snapping sound as he pulls the rest of her skin passed her feet sets me into a frenzy, jumpstarting my heart, it thunders inside my chest, filling my ears with the rush of blood. My legs wobble but don't move. My vision blurs and mouth dries.

He turns his attention to me now with his head cast down and his face hidden behind the hood. He raises it slowly and meets my stare. The strangers dark eyes are a richer color black than I've ever seen, a color that doesn't exist beyond those hollow holes.

He smiles, pulling his lips to expose his teeth, further than is possible, his cheeks tear and still the smile grows, ripping his face, blood pools in his mouth, turning his teeth a bloody crimson, it dribbles down his chin, his long tongue slithers out and laps it up. His eyes glued to mine, I see a hunger inside them that terrifies me.

And then he winks.

And I scream.

five

My entire body is shaking when I wake up on the couch, my lungs aching to breathe.

With trembling hands, I run my fingers through my hair, sweat dampened the strands making it sticky and a little painful.

My mouth feels dry as the desert and I can't swallow, although it feels like it would help the lump in my throat. I lean forward, elbows resting on my knees, and try to get my head level again.

It sounds weird as fuck but I know that monster in my dream saw me. I felt him see me. It was as if he saw inside of me. Those hollow dark eyes felt as though they could read my every thought.

I get up and grab a bottle of water, dribbles fall down the front of my shirt as I try to moisten my throat. I nearly choke but catch myself before I do.

With barely enough time to comprehend what the fuck that was, I see a brief movement in the ball, just a flicker, but it was enough to catch my eye.

I walk over to it and pick it up. There he is, his wide smile growing from my attention but this time it doesn't rip, instead he begins to speak.

It's hushed and I have to concentrate hard to hear him as it's not really spoken allowed. It doesn't feel as though someone in the room with me would be able to hear it. His words are only for me, I *feel* them rather than hear them, vibrating my bones, and tickling the hairs on my body.

"I thought I'd show you the kind of alternative fun Shelby should have had. You took David's kill from him. I wanted to show you it could have been much worse. Don't try and stop it. The demons of the world will have their fun."

He licks his lips slowly, top and then bottom, capturing it with his teeth, a cocky half grin and raised eyebrow the villains of the entertainment world always use to be sexy, completing his exhibition. And although I'm terrified, confused, and shocked, I'm also *wildly* turned on and the dryness in my throat has more to do with lust this time.

***

Something wakes me. A sensation more than anything, but it felt like someone had been touching me. My eyes are still closed, unable to move, I'm paralyzed--spine straight and tense.

I can swear there is someone in here. Someone who knows I am awake now and who's refusing to show them self to me. It smells like something unfamiliar.

I control my breathing, slowly in and out although every part of me begs to move.

Then, I feel it, the same touch that woke me, the fingers on my flesh, just the gentleness of fingernails smoothing over me. My skin reacts; goosebumps erupt.

My throat squeaks, a simple reactionary response to the strange sensation. I could swear I hear a chuckle, but my heart is beating too fast now to hear anything for sure. Even the tickle on my leg could be a figment happening only in a nightmare I simply thought I'd woken up from. But when I feel the warmth of the full palm on my calf I know there is no chance this is imagination at work.

It's warm, warmer than me, who is chilled from fright. A gentle squeeze from the fingers is nothing short of confusing. But before I have time to analyze it, the hand is on the move, traveling higher up my leg and between them. I want to close them, but fear won't allow me to move.

Isn't it supposed to be fight *or* flight? I guess they forgot the one where you could literally lose all control and probably die from immobility.

I'm on my tummy, like always, both hands tucked under my pillow with my face pointed toward the wall, a thin sheet covering some, but not all of me, and an oversized t-shirt doing me zero favors now as this stranger inches higher still, brushing lightly across the soft skin of my pussy.

You would think that that should trigger movement, but it doesn't, still nothing. I can't even swallow the lump in my throat.

Preparing for what might come next, I mentally tell myself that it should be over soon, he's only come here for sex and then he'll go, it will be over soon.

It will be over soon.

Fuck.

The mattress dips from his weight and I'm nowhere near ready to deal with this, even the voice in my head has the wherewithal to run and I'm left with only the silence.

He lifts my shirt upward, exposing more of my naked ass. I feel his hands on me harder now. Squeezing my cheeks, spreading them, manipulating as he wants.

A finger slides over my asshole and pushes subtly and with a quickness I'm not ready for, his tongue replaces it. Warm and wet he pushes it inside and around, nipping and caressing.

What the fuck?

Spreading my legs apart, without any resistance from me, his face moves lower, landing on the slit of my pussy, tongue gliding up and down, forcefully pushing against my clit.

My pulse thunders inside of me, sending a hot fire alight. Tensing my legs without instruction, I shiver my orgasm that couldn't be stopped even if I had my faculties. I know he feels it when his hot breath tickles me, reminding me of a chuckle.

Before I can make out what the actual fuck is going on, I hear the deafening sound of a zipper sliding down. Tooth by tooth. So slowly, I can almost count them. Feeling the pressure of his body move, I try one more time to force myself away from this, I've heard of night paralysis or whatever, but could it be that for this long? I don't have time to ponder any longer because now the pressure of him entering me seems more important.

Stretching me beyond comfort, the pain is abundant, I can almost thank him for the foreplay or I might be too dry to accommodate his dick. I can't quite count my blessings because the fullness I'm feeling is verging on too much.

Without effort, he tugs me upward onto my knees pushing into me so roughly it makes me lightheaded and pressing hard until sheathing himself fully.

Wrapping my hair inside his fist, he yanks it hard while he fucks me. Harder and faster, thighs slapping together until mine are stinging. I'm howling. He's grunting. Then I'm coming, the pressure inside me erupts and I can't hold anything back, the warmth of my release trickles down my legs and pools at my knees on my mattress.

The sloshing sound seems to encourage him. He fucks me harder and I only get wetter while my body is used and aching. He's a machine, pistoning inside of me faster and deeper, more of my own come pours from me like a waterfall as his hot, stickiness rushes inside my hole, collapsing heavily on top of me, flattening us both into my mess.

He brushes the hair off my forehead, dragging his tongue along my ear, sending a shiver across my skin.

"Wake up Sian," he breathes.

I can feel my body returning to me, the tingly sensations of pins and needles alert me to my limbs awakening.

He pulls his big cock out, inch by inch and so slowly I can feel it all, my pussy milking every last drop from him.

I don't know what happens for the next minute, but I wake up in my wet bed, in what can only be a moment later.

My pussy is aching, but the throb is not from pain, I'm so horny, I can't stop myself from tucking my arm under me and sliding my fingers through our hot mess, rubbing my clit until it dissipates and I get relief. It takes three orgasms before I am spent, nowhere near relieved, but close enough.

I don't blame myself for enjoying that, I've always been tempted toward the fucked up side of things.

I don't even hate myself when, after getting in the shower, the showerhead does me in one more time. Moaning, the name Lazlo on the tip of my tongue, barely escaping before I can bite it back.

I know that's his name, I don't know how I know. He hadn't told me, but it's perfectly clear that that was the smiling man I watched kill Shelby--kill being pretty toned down for what *actually* happened.

He had set fire to her secret rental condo, so it wasn't reported that she was skinned like a chicken breast, instead she was 'burned beyond recognition'.

Lazlo terrifies me, but absolutely turns me on. Maybe more than being afraid, I'm infatuated. I've never had my body, or my mind, owned like that before.

I just wish he hadn't worked whatever magic he has to paralyze me. I knew after I came the first time that it was probably him doing that, because I desperately wanted to push against him, fuck him back and show him that I wanted it.

Next time, I suppose.

I take my wobbly legs to work, sliding the key in the door but realizing it's not locked. I hesitate in the threshold when his smell hits me.

"Sian," he almost slithers my name, licking his top lip then sliding the bottom one through his teeth. My pussy clenches.

"Lazlo." I try to sound confident, as if I may have some authority. But the smile in his eyes heats my insides and makes me wet. Wetter.

“So, you heard it.” He comes up off the couch and reaches around me to shut the door, leaving me breathless. He pulls me toward him then takes a step back, putting a small breath of space between us. “Did you dream of me last night?” He traces a finger across my lips.

“Yes,” I squeak.

“Is that so?” he seems to contemplate this, his tongue toying with the back of his teeth, tilting his head from side to side while I struggle to hold his gaze.

I nod, blushing red.

“I’m curious, see… I’ve not been seen or heard in a very long time especially if I drag you to my side to have my way with you.”

I don’t think I’ve heard him right, and having him this close is overwhelming to every part of me. I take a step back, then another when it doesn't feel like enough.

"You may need to start at the beginning if you want me to understand you, especially if you're going to be confusing."

He takes a step toward me, but hesitates when he sees me making my retreat again. "Ok, the beginning. You ready? There is a place, like this one, kind of alongside it," he pauses. "Let me start over. You know those people that make you nervous, maybe you cross the street, avoid them, maybe you struggle to make eye contact with them? They have a place."

"Ok." I hurry him along with my hand, impatiently waiting for the punchline.

"Some people are born with a monster in them, something that makes them hard to look at, a hint of something unfamiliar to a normal person, it scares them, tingles their spine. The older the monster gets, or the more it's done monstrous things, the harder it is to look at, and when you stop being seen, you disappear. The other place takes you."

"So you're a monster then?" I'm only curious. I've felt like a monster a lot myself.

"You are one too. Only thing that makes sense to me."

I chuckle, "Oh, yea? Then why am I not in your other place?"

"It takes time, I told you, maybe you've not done enough. But you're coming."

"What's the worst thing you've done?" I don't mean to ask it, I don't know how to prepare for what he might say to me.

"Mmmm, curiosity killed the cat, little Sian," he almost purrs. This time he does close the gap, and the predatory way he approaches immobilizes me, he walks us both the wall, pressing me hard against it. "Well, kitty," tucking his hand up my skirt and inside my thin lace panties, he slips his finger inside me.

I'm embarrassed when I see him realize I'm so wet.

"I saw this woman, big round bellied pregnant woman. She made me...I don't know, interested." He pauses, fingering me faster. "I put my hand inside her. Ripped the baby out." Lazlo licks his lips, wetting them.

I can see he's aroused now, his eyes are black again. His fingers hook and he rubs that spot that I love. I put my hands on his shoulders to steady myself. And he leans down and puts his forehead against mine.

"She begged and panicked. She kept crying about her baby not being ready. So after I fucked her, I shoved the baby back inside of her."

I don't mean to, and it's almost like he planned it on purpose, but I come right then, hard and loud.

I feel him move, unable to open my eyes for now; I let him push me to my knees. His dick touches my lips and I open wide for him, tasting the precum that's beaded out. I open my eyes and look up at him as he pushes past my throat and starts fucking my face.

My head is pressed against the wall so I'm left to his discretion, tears rolling down my cheeks as I struggle to get breath into my lungs any chance I get. He's so big it feels like my cheeks are on the verge of ripping. It feels like it's all too much, but then he grabs my head on either side and fucks harder and even deeper. Snot, spit and tears cover my face and drip down my chin, it feels like I need to throw up, but my throat it too full to gag. The noises that I'm making are shameful. And it only encourages him.

"Oh, fuck Sian. I want to shoot this down your throat."

I struggle to nod, not really knowing if he's asking, but I want that too. One more deep thrust and then I feel him release deep inside my esophagus, squishing his balls hard against my chin.

He wipes the tears away from under my eyes before pulling his cock out so slowing I'm practically begging for air by the time he's done.

"Such a good messy little girl."

I lift the bottom of my shirt up and wipe my face on it, climbing off my knees.

"You might be the dirtiest monster there is, Sian."

"You confuse my body."

"That doesn't explain why you came when you did, now does it? You think you like what I did that to that woman? You wanna know the rest?"

"Yes...I think so."

I don't know.

"I slit her throat," his finger slides across my throat from one ear to the other, “and let the little one suffocate inside her.”

“Oh.” I feel the heat return to my tummy and the thing that is inside of me that loves the blood and the darkness of this is heating up, and I know Lazlo sees it turns me on.

“You’re getting so fucking hot for this aren’t you? I was right about you.”

“Was that the thing that made you go to the other place?” I walk over to the mini fridge and pull out two waters, handing him one and gently taking a sip of mine, knowing my throat will be raw for days.

“It’s not really one thing; it’s the culmination, or the desire, really. The more you have in you, the less people want you around, it just kind of happens.”

"Weird."

Another careful sip.

"Does it make you nervous for yourself? It doesn't hurt, it's not even boring, you just kind of flow between there and here. There, is where I took you and fucked you. For someone else, they may have had a flash that felt like remembering a dream. If anything. But for you, it's like you welcomed the journey."

"I couldn't move though, it felt like I was stuck, maybe paralyzed."

"Cool. I could have done anything to you."

"I remember you *doing* plenty of *anything* to me. Have you done that a lot?"

"No, I do what I want here, to these idiots, whatever I feel like doing. I couldn't help but want to explore you over there, it's different, but the same. I didn't want to fuck you up, but I guess it shouldn't have been a real concern." He plops down on the couch. "Do you remember it all?"

"I think so."

"Good."

I laugh.

"Do you actually need to be here today?"

"If you're asking if I have appointments for readings, then yes, I do."

"I'm gonna watch."

It should bother me, his abruptness, but it doesn't. "Will you have to hide?"

“No one can see me like you do. That’s not an exaggeration, if I’m in the other place, a few may be able to every now and then, but here, I’m like, invisible, only not really. If they focus on me, they can see me--if I let them, like if I want to interact, I could, but I only ever want to interact if I’m like cutting them or something,” a little laugh. “But overall I’m gone. People just stopped looking at me, started avoiding me. Then I just disappeared. I’m that thing you see in the corner of your eye, but when you look right at it, it’s not there. You can’t find me. People have trained themselves not to see the haunting things, the ghosts, whatever. I’m what churches call a demon. But without the dying part, and no cool possession. Just not of this world anymore.”

"Ok fine, you watch all you want. Do you think you'll be able to see what's in my ball?"

"I should, if you are getting real visions, which we both know you are, then it's from the other place. That's how I found you. I saw you peeking in. I've seen others do it too, but they've never seen me, they just see the premonition. So you get to be the special one."

He's joking and it seems like a rare look into this side of him. His eyes have color to them when he is like this, a green and amber mix. I like it almost as much as them black when he's fucking me.

Lazlo sits, arms wide on the top of the couch, one leg flung over the other, looking like he owns whatever he wants, when a petite brunette walks in with her daughter.

I put my hand out to shake hers and introduce myself, trying to keep my eyes focused on them and not on Lazlo. "I'm Sian."

"Brandy," she pushes the young girl forward and tells me her name is Charlotte."

I crouch down to her height. "Hi Charlotte, how old are you?"

"Eleven," she sets her shoulders back as if she's taking pride in being so old.

"That's a great age."

"I know."

I chuckle and see Lazlo lean forward with his elbow on his knee, becoming more interested. I didn't think he would be this enthralled, mostly I thought he'd be impatiently waiting for me to finish.

Brandy starts explaining what has brought them in today. "So, Charlotte here struggles a lot with the unknown. Recently her father died and now she must *know* that it won't happen to me."

Charlotte pulls her mother's arm.

"Or herself," Brandy continues, looking at me for forgiveness for her morbid questions.

"I completely understand your worries," I leave out that my mom also just died, because I think it might stress her out sharing such a thing, maybe making it all too common. "Come sit," I open my hand to them and direct them to the table, pulling an extra chair over for Brandy.

We are settled in, and after a quick flick of my eyes over to Lazlo, I start. "So is there anything else you'd want to talk about before we get to the big question?" I'm directing my question to Charlotte, but Brandy speaks up. "I'm wondering if I'm pregnant, I'm too nervous to take a test."

I pretend to get a response from the ball. "It doesn't look like it." Brandy's face shows her relief.

"See mama, I told you. It's just me and you."

I smile at Charlotte's jealousy.

"Can you just tell me please if my mama is going to die, I mean I know she will, but can you see if it will be soon, like when I'm still a young adult?"

The ball flickers as it always does when someone mentions death.

Brandy is driving on a rainy night. She's got grey hair, so I know for sure her death won't be soon, but I watch the rain hitting the windshield turn red and then she's no longer in a car. She's in my shop, and her face is blood covered and torn apart, she's howling as Lazlo rips Charlotte out of her seat and bites her cheek hard, tearing a piece of flesh away, spitting in on the ground and slamming her head hard into the table, splitting it open just before she flops onto the floor.

Still inside the ball, I watch Lazlo pull something from his pocket and gab it into Brandy's neck, dragging it along to the other side.

In a flash, and before I can rationalize what's happening, he makes it a reality in this time. The room is covered in blood, it's splattered across the ceiling from Brandy's squirting neck wound, the table has brain matter from the young girl now lying lifeless on the floor in her own puddle of it.

Lazlo, too, is covered in the mess, in slow motion I watch their blood dripping down his face and onto his shirt. He steps over Brandy to get to me, his black eyes growing larger and hungrier. Taking my wrist and pulling me into him, he presses his mouth to mine and shoves his tongue deep inside. I kiss him back, the heat growing between us. I smell the blood, taste the metallic copper of it, feel the stickiness, and I'm so wet.

He clears the table with a swipe of his arm then pushes my back onto it, hiking my skirt up and tearing hard at my panties until they rip away. He's inside if me quickly and it takes my breath away. He fucks me hard, lifting my legs and pushing behind my knees to open me up for him. The sweat coming from his forehead mingles with the blood and falls onto my face.

I don't know what compels me, but I drag my tongue up his cheek to collect it all and bring it into his mouth, kissing him--sharing it. It only makes him more ravenous.

Pulling my hair hard, he gains access to my neck where he drags his teeth along, sending a shiver through my body that's followed by an orgasm. What those teeth had just done to that little girls face in the back of my mind.

"Oh fuck, Lazlo," I moan, rocking my body with his as he slides me through the slick mess of carnage. Raking my nails down his back hard enough to break skin, we finish together, loud and sloppy, with his mouth on mine as we recover and catch our breath.

"That wasn't going to be her death," I both tell and ask him.

Shaking his head, his eyes light up and his eyebrows dance up and down. "I couldn't help it," he's not apologizing he's simply making a statement. He wanted something and he took it, his desire for it outweighing everything else.

"You just coudn't help yourself?" I bite my bottom lip, being flirty, "you just had to kill them," I push my pussy upward, meeting his not-so-soft cock, "and fuck me all over them?"

"Yea, you little fucking devil, I had to rip that little girl apart right in front of her mommy," he's fucking me again now, "then practically behead mom, because I fucking wanted to. And I wanted you to want me to do it."

"I liked it."

***

It took hours to get that room clean. If you knew what to look for you would be able to see the slight pink hue left behind on the ceiling, the missing rug under the table and the seam in the wood floor that is now a burnt red color from absorbing the blood into the grain.

It seems Lazlo knows most the tricks for clean up, he doesn't use them anymore, he told me, for the most part there is no need for him anymore. But while I'm still held to this world's rules for now, I have to play by them.

I still need to make a living and, honestly, I kinda like being able to see these things happen, sick as it sounds, it's been inside me since I was a little girl and it can finally flourish now.

After heading home, having thrown on one of my mom's heavy coats left in the shop's closet to make it there without getting noticed right away, I practically fall asleep before my head hits the pillow.

I wake with crusted blood over most my body, including my insides –I learn after getting in the shower, which takes so long before the water runs clear that I am out of hot water by the end.

I gladly take an appointment for noon today, excited to see what will come of it. Although Lazlo didn't come home with me last night, I have a sense that he's waiting at the shop for me this morning.

I throw on a cuter- than-necessary outfit just for him, thigh

high boots, with a nice heel, and a short skirt with something shear on top that I know you can see through. I want to make him squirm. And I suppose it wouldn't hurt too much if it improved my tip from the client.

Strange as it sounds, I smell him before I even open the door to the shop and the fact that it is stronger than the oils inside is saying a lot. He's sitting, looking sexy as fuck on the counter across the room from the main door.

"Mmmmm, hello there," he practically purrs.

"Lazlo," I say, setting my bag down, walking over to get inside his big arms.

"I could eat you right now, I'm absolutely insatiable."

I can't help but feel his words inside me. "You'll have to wait, I have a client coming in a less time than I'll want you to eat me." Giving him a flirty pout, I rub my hand over the front of his jeans, feeling the heat coming off them.

"Fine, but you're all mine after that," pinching my nipple through my top before he hops off the counter to sit on the couch. "Give me a good show, will ya?"

I don't know what I could possibly do to make it a good show for him, or even what he means by that, but my pondering is interrupted when the too- loud bell above the door chimes Richards arrival.

"Richard," I say, walking to the door to greet him.

His eyes drop to my bouncing tits, visible as if uncovered as the sunlight breaks in through the open door. He takes my extended hand but still hasn't brought his eyes to mine.

"I'm Sian," I say, wrapping his hand inside mine and guiding him to the table.

"Have a seat, tell me, what brings you in here today?" I sit across the small round table from him, propping my elbows on top and squeezing my D's together, since, it seems, that's all he has eyes for.

"Umm," he clears his throat, and then once more when still there are no words.

"Richard." I wait until enough time passes for him to realize he should be looking at me. He's an older man, maybe a few years younger than my mom, but still old enough to be my dad. Slightly grey, tall, a little fat and frumpy. Not to sound full of myself, but it seems he hasn't had a good look at someone like me in a long time.

"You married, Richard?" I ask when he finally meets my stare.

His affirmative head nod and his negative response make me giggle. "Does your wife know you're here?"

"She's the one who said I should come." He squirms in his seat almost embarrassed to say come.

"Tell me about her." I'm almost getting off on making him uncomfortable. I uncross my legs and spread them apart just enough that, should he look, he could see the little triangle of panty inside.

It takes him no time to drop his eyes, stuttering his response about his wife. I don't even listen as he stumbles through.

"Richard." Again, I'm left waiting for his eye contact, "is that your cock bulging your pants?"

Lazlo chuckles but I don't look over to him.

"Wha… no," his hand covers his fly as he makes more half words and excuses.

"So, if I were to ask you to show me that that isn't your dick, you'd be able to show me a flaccid, softy in there?"

"Yea, I mean, what, why would you?"

He honestly sounds like he wants to know why I'm asking, and right now, I really don't know, I think it's making me horny acting for these two men right now, teasing them both.

"I think I'm going to have to ask you to show me."

When all I get is his jaw on the floor, I reach over, scooting my chair along with me and grab his dick through his pants, hard. Squeezing so tightly he yelps. "Richard, what do you intend to do with this?"

"Um, nothing. I swear." He pulls at my wrist to remove my hand, but I start rubbing it and in no time he's hypnotized by the rhythm.

"You want me to stop?"

Shaking his head frantically he reaches his nervous hand toward me.

"You want to touch me?"

He gulps and nods his head.

Pulling my top over my head with my free hand, I watch as his pupils swell and I have to hold back a laugh.

Lightly grazing his hand across my chest, I moan for him. "Take your pants off, Richard."

Clumsy fingers fumble the button and the zipper; he nearly topples over getting his feet free. I take his dick in my hand before he sits down and massage it. I use a second to watch Lazlo release his own cock from of his pants, rock hard and excited.

"Oh Richard, you have a great cock. Does your wife tell you that?" he shakes his head.

I stand, pushing him down into his seat, "give me a second," before he's able to respond, I walk away into the bathroom but I'm back in a flash.

Unfastening my skirt and letting it slide down my hips as I walk back toward him, leaving me in the tiniest thong. I wait until I'm in front of him to remove it, tossing it onto his lap and then resting my ass against the table and spreading my legs wide, I take his head and pull his face to my pussy. "Eat me Richard."

As Richard fumbles his way through, I watch Lazlo pump his own cock, staring me right in the eyes with his so black they twist my tummy.

Rocking myself hard against Richards face, grabbing his hair too hard for his comfort, I nearly come from my own arousal rather than anything he's actually doing with is mouth.

"Good boy, Richard." His tongue stays right where I need it to be for long enough to reach my finish.

“I want to fuck you,” he manages, my come wet on his chin.

“I know that, silly.” Sliding off the table and onto my knees, I grab his dick and pump it hard, he’s probably harder than he’s ever been, it looks painful. I lick the tip and he practically cries out. “You like that?”

“Yes,” he says, looking down at me with eager eyes, begging me to keep going. I stick my tongue out again and he moves toward it, barely reaching me as I slice through the shaft at the base- that sweet spot under his balls that’s like butter. I suck his dick into my mouth and he comes before he even feels the pain, possibly only noticing what I’ve done when he watches me remove it from my mouth unattached to him.

Balling up the come in my mouth, I spit it on the table. “That was crazy; you're supposed to tell a girl when you're ready to nut."

Stammering, looking from his cock and balls in my hand, down to his bloody crotch and back again, unable to conger actual words. I take advantage of this confusing time to get behind him and hoist him up and onto the table. He doesn't even struggle, just folds over it.

"You still want me to fuck you, Richard?" Covering his dick with my spit, rubbing it down the shaft, I line it up with his ass and shove hard. It goes in easier than I thought it would.

Lazlo is quick on his feet. "Oh my god, you are my favorite monster," his mouth comes down hard on mine and he fucks my tongue.

The groaning from Richard is becoming more of a whine and

fainter as his blood pools onto the floor. Without my help, he slides down the table and onto his stomach, hitting the floor sloppily, his dick slipping out of his butt on impact, hitting the floor like a rubber dong.

Lazlo replaces the empty spot on the table with me, bending me forward, entering me hard and fast. I'm lost in it until I feel a hot sensation on my back, then more. It's hot only for a second the it fizzles out and I realize he's dipping the candle wax on me.

"You're a good fucking slut, Sian, makes me want to fuck this little asshole. But I like it in your pussy so much too."

I feel the pressure at my ass and try to relax as he pushes the candle inside me and then fucks both holes hard. We both come, loudly. I'm almost too weak to stand, but I have to, because Richard still needs to die.

"Richard," I say.

He moans.

"You gotta go now," twisting his arm and flopping him onto his back, I straddle his thick body. "You still wanna fuck, Richard? Let's fuck." I ride him with mock- exaggerated excitement and bounce on his lap as if I'm fucking him, "aw, now it's no fun." I whine. "Oh well, no last hooray for you, I guess," I put my finger in the air, "unless," I reach for his amputated cock, "you could fuck yourself in your new pussy." I push hard and his dick slides into the cavity that's been left behind. Pulling it in and out, "see I can fuck you soooo good."

I leave it in him and reach for the razor I took from the bathroom and hid inside my boot, I plunge it into his neck, digging deep to cut the veins. Before removing it, I cover the wound with my hand so we don't have to spend too much time on the ceiling now. It works, and the spray is interrupted before it reaches that far.

"Good thinking," Lazlo says sarcastically.

It makes me laugh. "We really need to start laying tarps down or some shit.

"Oh, my sweet Sian, you won't need to worry about that much longer if you aren't careful." I think I know what he's implying—that I'll be in the other place in a matter of time if I keep this up, but I can't stop myself, and I don't want to. I want to spend forever being Lazlo's monster sidekick.

"I want this."

"Oh yea, you want to just leave this world, and all the people in it, and move over to the other place. Forever? There's no redemption—nothing, no changing your mind, once people don't want you here, you don't get to be here anymore. It's *forever*, and I mean the *real* forever, like *eternity*."

I nod, half listening. "Why does your face look like it does in the ball? When you looked at me and smiled, I could swear your face split open and bled." I've been dying to ask and since he's speaking freely, I decide to ask.

"Like this?" He smiles the sexy smile I've seen so often recently and then stretches it, turning his eyes black, with a snarling nose, and just like before, his cheeks rip apart and I see all his teeth cover in blood. My heart thunders inside my chest and then goes wild watching him take his top lip and rip his face up, revealing his skull, his blackened eye winks at me. And then, his flirty smile is back and he's normal again. "I don't know why it happens, honestly. It's pretty cool though, huh?" He looks so excited to be sharing this with me. "We don't really have human rules, their world is safe and full of fluffy things, and the other place is only nightmares and monsters."

"I think I used to dream of the other place when I was younger. It would make all my dreams bloody and scary, only it never really scared me. I actually masturbated for the first time after waking up, covered in sweat, remembering the brutal way some man had killed a woman. He was slicing her up and I couldn't help but watch, loving it all. I wasn't able to keep my hands off of myself after that."

Lazlo comes closer to me, covered in Richard's dried blood, and moves a crusted piece of hair away from my forehead and presses his to mine. "You are gonna be stuck with me for a long fucking time. I'm not letting your sick ass go. So, you also ready for that?"

"Yep. Let's fuck some shit up so I can *demonized*." We laugh and begin our tedious clean up, hopefully there won't be many more of these, but it will be fun either way.

six

Walking alone through downtown has me feeling a little out of sorts. Typically, I would be getting men's attention, they'd be looking at me hopeful for a little smile from me, but I'm getting none of it. I begin watching more closely and I can almost see a flinch before they turn away. Lazlo wasn't wrong, I think people are beginning to ignore me, to look away from me.

Standing directly in the path of a group of people, playing chicken, if you will, not a single one looks directly at me, it's almost as if they part for no real reason and none of them wonder why.

It's actually kind of exhilarating. Being unseen could have many advantages and I like all the ideas I have in my mind.

Lazlo meets me at the theatre and we watch a movie. Some horror flick that is full of boobs and blood.

My favorite.

"Most people aren't seeing me anymore." I say after the movie, on our walk back to my place.

"Uhh, duh, you're a freak now," he laughs and grabs my hand, "couldn't happen to a nicer girl."

I roll my eyes at him. "It feels weird, going from the focal point to being avoided, it's like I have broccoli stuck in my teeth and no one wants to tell me."

"Yea, I'm sure that's super accurate," I can hear his sarcasm and I pretend to glare at him.

"It's strange, is all I mean."

"Tell me about it, imagine if I hadn't told you about it, suppose you just ended up in the middle of the darkest room and no one could hear you, you just wander--possibly for years--until someone finally looks. That's what I had happen. A random demon told me what was happening. And, don't get me wrong, I wasn't wallowing at all, I took full fucking advantage of what was happening to me. I think that's why the demons weren't even noticing me. They're all levels, some shy away from the worse ones there too."

"Wow, that would be fucking weird." I stop short and look him in the eyes. "I don't know what it says about me that I could see you--this *horrible* monster, and me, just a poor little human girl," I feign an innocence I've never had.

He leans in and puts his mouth to mine, "it says you're a fucking demon, *my* demon. Now, let's fuck some shit up. I have just the place."

I follow as best I can in the tall heels I'm in as he drags me by my hand into a darkened alley. Once there, we walk slower, keeping our steps silent until a building comes into view and then he halts us so he can explain that we are here to ruin these kids.

“It’s a crack house, these fuckers are all sorts of messed up. It’s super fun to mess with people on drugs. I’ll show you.”

I watch Lazlo do his thing, following a little further back to be more an observer. Tingles of excitement are nonstop flowing, it’s like every cell of my body is producing goosebumps of their own.

He creeps into the building, ducking under a low hung two by four to keep people out, looks like the rest had been yanked down long ago.

The large loft- style building is dark, save for the single flickering candle lit by the group of whispering teens, looks to be about seven of them, huddled together in the far corner.

“Whatcha doing in here?” A voice booms in the silence, startling even me, and then echoes for so long it hurts my ears.

The kids all turn to Lazlo as he quickly approaches them. Scurrying to get to their feet, but not being the most level headed for the task, they are left frozen, waiting for Lazlo to continue his inquiry.

“I said,” he keeps his voice lower so he’s not left waiting for the echoes to cease. “What are you doing here? Having fun, hanging with your friends, doing drugs… fucking?”

“No, sir, none of that, we’re just vibing,” one of the more brave boys says.

“Oh, cool, they’re just vibing, babe.” It seems only I’m able to hear the mocking tone. He looks over at me and I see the kids turn in my direction, but because the light from the candle doesn’t reach this far, they can't see me. I stay hidden in the darkness.

"I think you kids should go--before I have to *make* you." Lazlo steps slowly toward them, growing a giant shadow on the wall, and then, just an arm's length away, he yells, "ruuuuuun." And I don't know how they manage it, but they do, shaking the confusion away, fumbling on their feet, like hell is nipping at their heels, they quickly dart to the farthest corner of the building and escape through a secret looking cubby hole.

Lazlo moves quickly, not running, almost like Michael Myers—no doubt he is going to catch up to them.

I get through the cubby right after Lazlo, and find we are in a meadow. There are flowers, full, colorful, and brightly lit by multiple giant security motion lights, the kids setting each of the next ones off as they run further away.

The meadow is familiar, and as I walk through it, trying to recall the reason for my déjà vu, I'm hit with it, only it is the bloody bodies, and not the flowers, that bring it back. My recurring dream from childhood--it's happening right now. The meadow, fully lit up by countless watts of light and the soon to be seven teen bodies brutally taken down by Lazlo and possibly myself.

It's my first vision. I just didn't know it was a vision until now, this was always my path, my calling, or fucking destiny. Whatever. But if there was any shred of apprehension about what I'm becoming, and the chance that I might regret it, it's gone now. This vision had shaped me in more ways than one and it has become me, or I have become it?

So when I hear Lazlo catch up to one of them, the frightened scream of the girl being captured, I run toward it. Setting eyes on her, a huge fucking grin on my face, I see her reaction to me and it widens. I can feel it tearing my cheeks and she wails, struggling to escape Lazlo, who I know is seeing me too. My monster lunges at her and rips her face apart with my teeth.

The warmth of it floods my mouth, I taste her fear--I know people say that, but I can seriously taste the sweetness of her terror, and I'm ready for a sugar high.

Lazlo reaches for my face and licks her blood off of me, and then we both dive in again, tearing her apart, the sinew and flesh coming away easily. I carry her severed head by her hair, wrapped tightly around my fingers, as we go searching for the rest of her friends.

Lazlo stops abruptly, eyes closed and nose in the air, almost as if he can smell them. I do it to, focusing on the sweetness. The wind swirls or changes direction and we both seem to find it at the same moment.

We move quickly, but quietly, stalking toward the general direction of the smell, it seems to get stronger the closer we get to them.

There is a grouping of bushes off to one end of the field, and if I was in the mood to place a bet, I'd put it on that.

We find four of them there, three girls and a boy, huddling so tightly they look as if they're trying to morph together, or like a school of fish, appear larger than they are.

"Hey," I whisper directly into the boy's ear. The shriek he makes when he realizes I've made it this close without him realizing sends a chill into my bones.

He screams again when I drag him out of the huddle by his hair.

Lazlo pounces on the stack of remaining girls, I listen to the crunching of their bones, the ripping of their skin, and if I focus hard enough, I think I can hear a soft humming purr coming from him.

I put my nose to the boy and take a deep whiff, making my way around his entire body, enjoying all the different scents he has created. I can smell the sweetness of fear, the earthiness of his sweat, the iron of his quick flowing blood. They mingle together and hits right between my thighs.

I tear his pants off when I find I like the smell best down there, moving my tongue around his flesh, swirling and tasting. Wrapping my mouth around his balls and then his cock, I fit them both inside and then wiggle my tongue.

Looking up at him, I notice the confusion on his face as the biology of his body tells him to enjoy this, but his brain tells him to run.

I suck harder, slowly up and down until his cock is hard and his eyes show me his enjoyment. I feel the purr in the back of my throat, and crunch down. The sweet flow of blood pulses out and he screams, trying to fumble his way out of my reach, but I climb up his body, gripping his wrists tightly over his head.

Licking his blood from around my mouth with a long grotesque demon tongue, I show him the taste of it, pushing it into his mouth, forcing it to grow and worm its way further down his throat, then fuck him with it.

His eyes bulge in horror, unable to breathe around my too-long tongue. I release his hands and pull on his top and bottom jaw, slowly applying the pressure needed to tear them apart.

The top of his head doesn't come off like I was hoping, but his top jaw sits in my hand, still attached to his face by the skin of his nose. After a quick yank, it comes away like a pesky hangnail.

Lazlo finishes his kills and I watch him approach, completely drenched in so much blood, only the whites of his blackened- iris eyes are not maroon. He smiles at me, watching me toss the kids teeth away, my monster tongue fucking the life out of him.

“Sian,” he moans, “you may just be the wickedest of us all.

I retract my tongue with a flick back into my mouth, all three feet of it returning to normal after I want it to and I use it to answer him. “Thanks, babe.” I shouldn’t, but I take pride in that.

“Off to the grand finale? By my count there are two more.”

“Oooh, let’s go.” Climbing off the very dead boy, I grab Lazlo for help to my feet and then we take off in pursuit of our next.

The last two are surprisingly easy to find, I don’t think very highly of them, knowing they have had the most time to run or hide, they've chosen neither successfully. Fucking morons, the last girl and boy are at the far end of the field, sitting perfectly still as we approach them, not hidden behind anything, and mostly hoping, it looks, that they would have been forgotten about.

I stop Lazlo before he reaches them, turning him away from them so I can tell him what I want from him. "I really want you to fuck her and make it hurt."

"I can do that." He takes my hand and shoves it down the front of his pants; I massage his cock until it's swollen and ready for her.

With a quickness the poor girl wasn't expecting, he is on her, tearing her clothes off and pushing into her. The boy keeps his stone-like position, doing even less moving, if that were even possible.

Lazlo shoves his dick inside her, "bigger, make it bigger." I plead.

"My dick?" he asks, confused.

"Yea, like I made my tongue big, make that big cock of yours even bigger, I want you to split her open."

She howls as he grows, pulling out I can see the blood on his giant dick before it goes back inside of her, it's tearing her up, and destroying her insides.

"Harder, Lazlo. Fuck her. Come that big dick load inside of her."

After a few more brutal thrusts I know he finishes when I see the come ooze from her eyes, spilling from her mouth and nose in bubbling cream. She's dead for sure before she has to suffocate on it.

Lazlo drags his massive pole, thicker than the girl's thigh, out of her and slowly it returns to its normal size and shape.

"I didn't even think of doing anything like that before, Sian. This opens a completely new level of shit we are going to do. You have no idea how excited I am for this. You are fucking brilliant and twisted as fuck."

"Well, if you could save all that sweet talk for after I've had mine, that would be best, my pussy is dripping, and that boy needs to fuck me."

He kisses me quickly, "by all means, you fuck that boy raw, give me a good show."

I pull my shorts down, kicking them aside as I approach him. His head shakes wildly, begging me to come no further.

"Not to worry, kid, this is gonna to be so fun, I promise."

"But, but…but…" he keeps his eyes on me, pointing at his friend, come covering her face like a fancy facial mask.

"That's not going to happen to you, I don't even have a dick." Gripping his dick in my fist I tug hard. "Come on, you can get hard for me, can't you? My pussy is so wet, let me have this dick."

It doesn't get hard, but the blood is definitely working south, its barely above soft when I straddle him and shove what I can into me. Rocking gently on him, I can feel it grow, although he doesn't want it to. Gaining more rhythm, I grind his lap deeper and deeper, its filling me so full and I still want more. I dig deeper and grid harder, faster until it stretches my hole, shoving more of him inside, my pussy widening to accept more, and then more.

I continue to fuck him until there is no more of him and I envelope every inch of his body inside me like a snake eating its meal. I finally come, so hard my pussy so juicy, it expels him right back out, dripping wet and in a creamy, sloppy mess, bones broken and misshapen.

I lie back, utterly spent.

Looking to Lazlo, reaching for his hand as my head lands heavy on the ground.

“I guess she was hungry,” he laughs.

“Yea.”

After catching my breath we make it to our feet, I take a quick glance around at the mess that we

have made of the beautiful flowers.
This is exactly what I was made for.

The end

Thank you for reading

More by Rayne

Boys Will Be Boys

Collecting Rayne
(a collection of the first 8 stories,
including)

My Christmas Story

The Boy

Degenerate

Devour

Retaliation

XXX

app

The Embalmer

Printed in Great Britain
by Amazon